On the Trapline

Written by

DAVID A. ROBERTSON

Illustrated by

JULIE FLETT

tundra

I'm on my way up north because Moshom, my grandpa, is taking me to his trapline. I've never been there before, and Moshom says he hasn't been since he was a kid like me. When I look out the window, all I can see are trees and water. The lakes look like blue clouds in a green sky.

“What’s a trapline?” I ask.

“Traplines are where people hunt animals and live off the land,” he says.

When we touch down in the community, Moshom's old friend is waiting for us.

"Tansi," he says to Moshom.

"Tansi," Moshom says to him. Moshom speaks Swampy Cree when he's around friends.

"Hi," I say. That's what tansi means in English.

It’s different here. In the city everything’s all bunched up. In the north there’s so much space. Moshom says relatives live in houses close to each other, but to me it looks like there’s still lots of room between them.

Kīwētinohk means “north.”

We pull up to a small house beside a big lake.

"Is this your trapline?" I ask.

"No," Moshom says. "This is where we lived after we left the trapline."

Moshom tells me that in the winter, everybody in the family slept in one room, where the wood stove kept them warm. He says it was nice being together like that. I guess some things are bunched up in the north.

Wakomakanak means "family."

We walk to the shore behind the house. There are all kinds of rocks. Big and small, round and flat. I think about the beach I go to near the city, where there's only sand.

"This is where we used to swim," Moshom says.

Moshom tells me that he and his brothers and sisters made paper boats here too. They would pretend the boats were freighters and put tiny rocks in them to see how long they would float.

Kapasimo means "swim."

We drive down a gravel road that winds through trees, like a snake. At the end of the road, a path leads to the remains of an old building.

"This is where I went to school after we left the trapline," Moshom says. "Most of the kids only spoke Cree, but at the school all of us had to talk and learn in English."

"Did you still get to speak Cree?" I ask.

"My friends and I snuck into the bush so we could speak our language," he says.

Ininīmowin means "Cree language."

We look at the birch trees and pine trees and all the long grass. I imagine Moshom and his friends speaking Cree in there.

“Is that your trapline?” I ask.

“No,” he says. “My trapline is far from here.”

I ask Moshom what it was like going to school after living on the trapline. He is quiet for a long time.

“I learned in both places,” he says. “I just learned different things.”

Pahkan means “different.”

There's a river at the end of the highway. We get into one of the motorboats docked along the shore and head out onto the water. The river is wide, but Moshom's smile is even wider.

Moshom tells me his family's boat only had a one horsepower putt-putt engine.

“That’s not a lot of horses,” I say, but I think it would be nice to travel slow around here.

Pēhkach means “slowly,” and minwasin means “beautiful.”

I see all kinds of things. Beaver dams, eagles flying overhead and paintings on rocks. I see the sun climb higher and shadows get shorter. I see blue water turn to black. That's when Moshom's eyes light up.

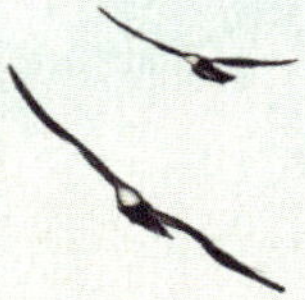

He points to a boulder by some thick trees.

"That's my trapline," he says.

Kīwēw means "he goes home."

Moshom needs a walking stick, so I find him a perfect piece of driftwood.

“This is where we lived when we were on the trapline,” he says.

Moshom tells me that everybody in the family slept in one big tent, so they could keep warm at night. I think it would’ve been nice, being together like that.

Pahkwanikamik means “tent.”

We find a pile of wood that looks like a giant game of pick-up sticks.

“This is where we chopped wood,” he says.

Moshom tells me that even the youngest children had jobs to do, and everyone would share the work. I think about my chores back in the city. Putting away dishes. Cleaning up my room. I wonder what it would be like to do my chores outside instead.

Wanawī means “go outside.”

There are bushes all around the clearing. We find one that's full of saskatoon berries. Moshom picks one and puts it right into his mouth.

"When we were hungry, we had to find food," he says. "We ate all kinds of berries."

I pick a saskatoon berry and eat it just like Moshom. It tastes better than the fruit we get at the store. I have more than just one.

Mīnisa means "berries."

We walk together, back to the shore. Moshom tells me that this is one of the places where he used to set traps. He caught all kinds of animals, but mostly rats.

"You mean like the ones that live in sewers?" I ask. I've seen that kind of rat on television.

"No," he laughs. "Muskrats."

Moshom tells me they ate the muskrat meat. The pelts were sold to buy flour, tea, sugar and lard — things you couldn't get on the trapline.

Pisiskowak means "animals."

When we're about to leave, I stand with Moshom by the lake.

He holds my hand tight, but he doesn't say anything.

Kiskisiw means "he remembers."

We stop to fish on the way back. Moshom's friend catches lots of fish. Moshom catches some. I almost catch one, but it gets away.

"Why are you so good at fishing?" I ask.

“We used to fish on the trapline too,” he says.

Moshom tells me that we can share. On the trapline, everybody shared with everybody else.

Natinamakēwin means “sharing.”

That night, the community has a feast. There's bannock, mixed vegetables, berries, wild meat and all the fish we caught. It makes my stomach rumble.

Moshom is an Elder. After he blesses the food, it's my job to serve him his meal. Elders get to eat before anybody else.

"Ekosani," he says when I bring his food.

Ekosani means "thank you."

When it's time to go home to the city, I ask Moshom if we can come back soon. He says that we can. After we take off, I see Moshom looking out the window.

"Can you see your trapline?" I ask.

"Yes," he says. "I can imagine it just the way it used to be, and just the way it is. Can you?"

Wapahtam means "he sees it."

I close my eyes and picture the trapline. The trees, the water and all the land and little islands. Chopping wood and picking berries. Catching rats at the shore, but not that kind of rat. Sleeping in a tent with family to stay warm. Standing by the lake with Moshom.

I open my eyes.

"Yes," I say. "I can see it too."

A Note from the Author

My father grew up on the trapline, from the time he was born until he was nine years old, when he and his family moved to Norway House permanently. After that, he went with his father intermittently, but by his mid-teens he left the trapline for what seemed the last time. Then, in the summer of 2018, Dad and I headed out onto the land together. He hadn't been for seventy years. It was the first time for me.

Reconciliation is more than just healing from trauma. It's connecting, or reconnecting, with people, culture, language, community. Being on the trapline with my father was the most significant moment in our relationship — a homecoming for me as a Cree man and truly a journey home for him.

DAVID A. ROBERTSON

A Note from the Illustrator

I was thrilled to be asked to work on a story about David and his father. David's mom and dad are dear to me. Some of my own family come from Norway House Cree Nation, the same community that David's family comes from. My family worked in the fur trade. My grandfather and great-uncles were trappers and traders, hunters and fishers. My grandmothers beaded and sewed mittens, parkas, vests, leggings and moccasins made from caribou and deer hide. My father hunted as a young boy to bring food home for his family. Though I missed out on experiencing many of these traditions, I'm happy to see that my son and nieces have since learned the skills for living on the land. They're learning their grandparents' languages, and my niece beads like her grandmothers did.

JULIE FLETT

Kisākihitin, Dad. You are home. — DAR

Kinanâskomitin, Dad, for the love and the sweetgrass. In loving memory, Clarence Flett, Swampy Cree, Red River Métis (1936 - 2019). — JF

Tundra Books, an imprint of Penguin Random House Canada Young Readers, a division of Penguin Random House of Canada Limited

Library and Archives Canada Cataloguing in Publication

Title: On the trapline / David A. Robertson ; [illustrations by] Julie Flett.
Names: Robertson, David, 1977- author. | Flett, Julie, illustrator.
Identifiers: Canadiana (print) 20200212060 | Canadiana (ebook) 20200212109
ISBN 9780735266681 (hardcover) | ISBN 9780735266698 (EPUB)
Classification: LCC PS8585.O32115 O5 2021 | DDC jC813/.6—dc23

Published simultaneously in the United States of America by Tundra Books of Northern New York, an imprint of Penguin Random House Canada Young Readers, a division of Penguin Random House of Canada Limited

Library of Congress Control Number: 2020936825

Acquired by Tara Walker
Edited by Debbie Rogosin and Elizabeth Kribs
Designed by John Martz
The artwork in this book was rendered in pastel on paper, and then composited digitally.
The text was set in Circular Pro.

Printed and bound in China

www.penguinrandomhouse.ca

1 2 3 4 5 25 24 23 22 21

tundra | Penguin Random House TUNDRA BOOKS

The Swampy Cree words in this story are:

Moshom (moo-shum): Grandpa

Tansi (tan-see): Hello

Kīwētinohk (kee-way-tin-awk): North

Wakomakanak (wah-co-mack-ah-nack): Family

Kapasimo (kah-pah-sim-oh): Swim

Ininīmowin (in-in-ee-mo-win): Cree language

Pahkan (pa-can): Different

Pēhkach (bay-catch): Slowly

Minwasin (min-wah-sin): Beautiful

Kīwēw (kee-way-oh): He goes home

Pahkwanikamik (pa-kwah-nick-ah-mick): Tent

Wanawī (wah-nah-wee): Go outside

Mīnisa (mean-ih-sa): Berries

Pisiskowak (pih-sis-co-wack): Animals

Kiskisiw (kis-kis-su): He remembers

Natinamakēwin (nah-tin-ah-mah-kay-win): Sharing

Ekosani (ay-co-zah-nee): Thank you

Wapahtam (wah-pa-tam): He sees it